Jim Henson's
DINOSAUR TRAIN

Dinosaur Egg Day!

Adapted by Maggie Testa

Based on the screenplay "The Nursery Car" written by Corey Powell

Based on the television series created by Craig Bartlett

SIMON SPOTLIGHT

An imprint of Simon & Schuster Children's Publishing Division

New York   London   Toronto   Sydney   New Delhi

1230 Avenue of the Americas, New York, New York 10020

This Simon Spotlight paperback edition December 2017

Manufactured in the United States of America 1117 LAK · 10 9 8 7 6 5 4 3 2 1

ISBN 978-1-5344-1171-5 (pbk) · ISBN 978-1-5344-1172-2 (eBook)

It was a very special day. There was a new car on the Dinosaur Train! The Pteranodon family couldn't wait to see it.

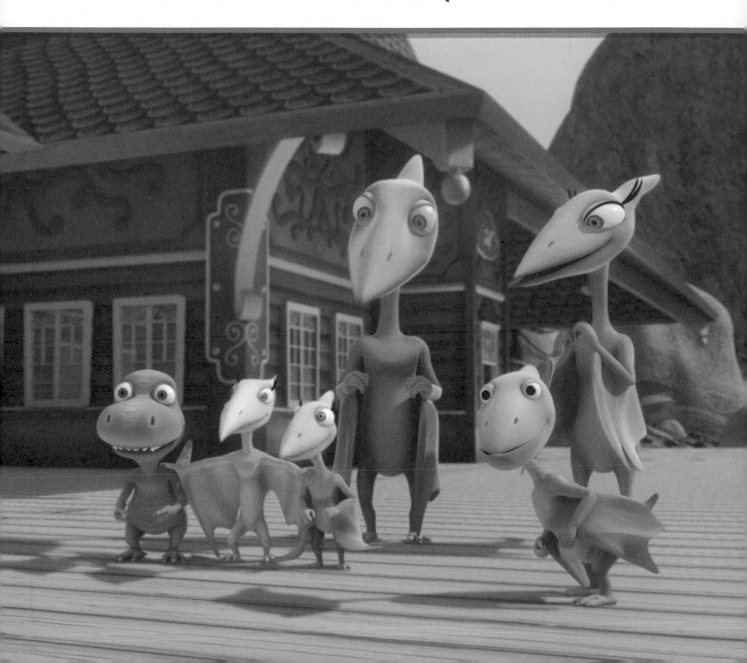

"Greetings," said Mr. Conductor as the Pteranodon family found their seats. "Welcome aboard the very first run of our special new car, the nursery car!"

The nursery car had nests filled with dinosaur eggs. Soon the eggs would hatch, and baby dinosaurs would come out.

"It seems like so long ago since my four babies were tiny little eggs," said Mrs. Pteranodon, thinking back to when Buddy, Tiny, Shiny, and Don's eggs hatched.

In the nursery car, the Pteranodon family saw dinosaur parents watching over their nests.

There were Velociraptor parents, Triceratops parents, Maiasaura parents, and Troodon parents.

"I wonder which eggs go with which parents," said Buddy. "All these eggs kind of look alike."

Back when Buddy and his siblings' eggs hatched, Buddy's egg looked different from the others. As he grew, Buddy looked different too. That's because he is a Tyrannosaurus rex and they are Pteranodons. Even so, Buddy knows that some kids look like their families, and some don't. All that matters is that his family loves him!

"Let's see," said Tiny. "I think the little eggs might belong to Mrs. Triceratops and the yellow ones might be Mrs. Troodon's, but I'm not really sure."

Buddy had a different thought. "Since Triceratops is such a big dinosaur, I bet the bigger eggs are Triceratops."

Shiny had another question. "How do the babies breathe in their eggs?" she asked.

Buddy had an idea. "The eggshells must be thin enough for the babies inside to breathe the outside air."

"But they still must be really strong so they don't crack before the babies are ready to hatch," added Tiny.

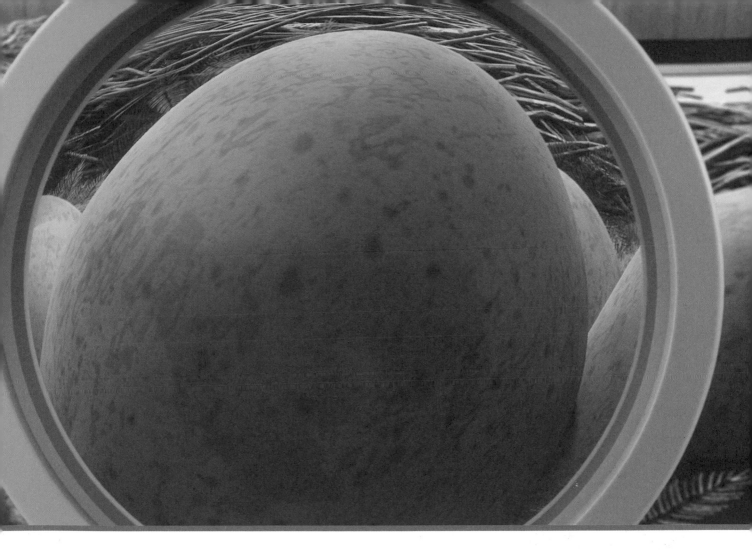

"You're both right," said Mr. Conductor, taking out his magnifying glass. "If you look closely, you can see lots of tiny holes in the shells. Those are called *pores*."

"I don't remember being in an egg," said Don, "but I like breathing."

A few seconds later, all the eggs started to move.
"They're hatching!" Buddy, Tiny, Shiny, and Don cheered.

It was true. The eggshells were cracking, and baby dinosaurs were starting to peek out of them. All the dinosaurs in the nursery car were very excited, especially the soon-to-be new moms and dads!

After the eggs hatched, Buddy and Tiny visited each of the baby dinosaurs.

"Look at those teeny feathers," Tiny said about the Velociraptor babies.

"It'd be fun to compare the babies' features to their parents'," said Buddy.

Tiny agreed. So did Mr. Conductor. "Compare and contrast," he said. "And remember, dinosaur newborns often look different from their parents, with bigger eyes and rounder faces."

Buddy and Tiny could see that Mr. Conductor was right. The Triceratops baby looked like his parents, but not exactly. He didn't have horns yet—just little nubs where horns would grow as he got older.

The baby Troodon looked just like his mom and dad, only smaller. He even had a teeny-tiny toe claw.

The Maiasaura baby had little fingers and little teeth!

And the baby Velociraptor had feathers, but not as many as his mom. Someday he would!

The older these babies got, the more they would look like their parents.

"But all of them start from little eggs!" said Buddy.

"Correct, Buddy," said Mr. Conductor. "Even the biggest dinosaurs hatch out of a small egg."

The Pteranodon family had a great day on the Dinosaur Train, but they had one more thing to do. They made a special "We love you, Mom" present. All four kids put their footprints in a slab of mud and gave it to Mom.

"Now you can remember us when we were this big," said Tiny.

"One day, we'll be older and bigger, and I'll be a giant T. rex," said Buddy. "Roar!"

"Thank you, kids," said Mrs. Pteranodon. "It doesn't matter how big you are, you'll always be my little babies."

"Group hug!" shouted Shiny.

DINOSAUR DATA

ALL ABOUT EGGS!

Eggs are small, but they're very important. Every dinosaur that ever lived hatched from an egg. Even the biggest dinosaurs started out as little eggs.

When dinosaur parents were waiting for their eggs to hatch, they put them in nests, just like birds do today. There could have been as many as 20 to 25 eggs in a nest.

And there were more eggs nearby! Dinosaurs made their nests near other nests, creating a colony. Colonies helped protect the eggs from predators.

ALL ABOUT DINOSAUR FOOTPRINTS!

What do footprints tell us about dinosaurs? A lot! A long time ago, dinosaurs made tracks in mud, and those tracks were preserved, or fossilized. Scientists study those fossils today. Fossil footprints have been found on all seven continents. That's Africa, Antarctica, Asia, Australia, Europe, North America, and South America!